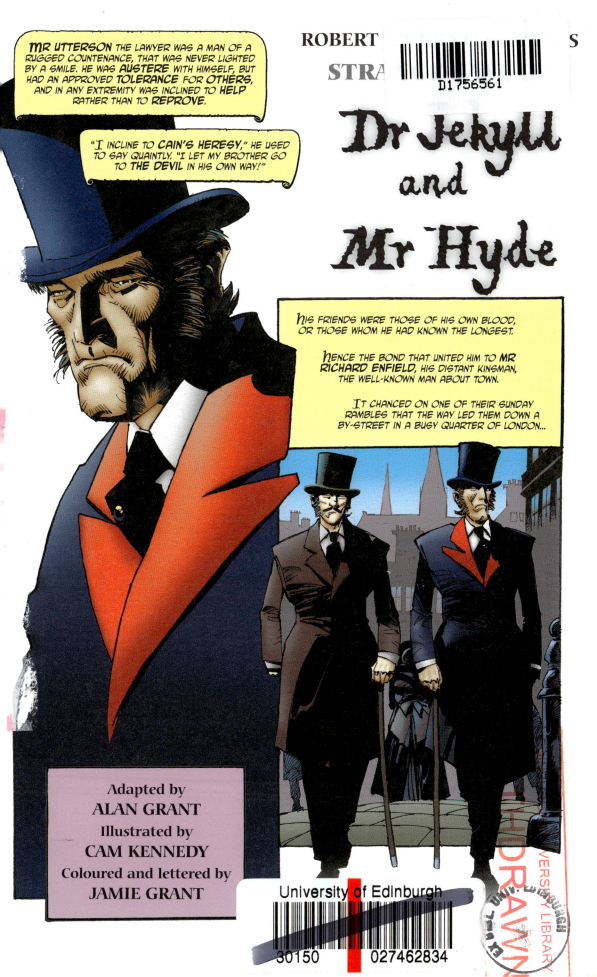

"ALL AT ONCE I SAW TWO FIGURES: ONE A **LITTLE MAN** WHO WAS STUMPING ALONG EASTWARD AT A GOOD WALK..."

"AND THE OTHER A **GIRL** OF MAYBE EIGHT OR TEN, RUNNING AS HARD AS SHE WAS ABLE DOWN A CROSS STREET."

"THE TWO RAN INTO ONE ANOTHER AT THE CORNER."

"AND THEN CAME THE **HORRIBLE** PART OF THE THING..."

"FOR THE MAN **TRAMPLED** CALMLY OVER THE CHILD'S BODY AND LEFT HER **SCREAMING** ON THE GROUND!"

YOU, SIR!

I HAD TAKEN A **LOATHING** TO MY GENTLEMAN AT FIRST SIGHT. SO HAD THE CHILD'S FAMILY, WHICH WAS ONLY NATURAL. BUT THE **DOCTOR**...

EVERY TIME HE LOOKED AT MY PRISONER, THAT SAWBONES TURNED **WHITE** WITH THE DESIRE TO **KILL** HIM!

"**I** NEVER SAW A CIRCLE OF SUCH **HATEFUL** FACES."

"**A**ND THERE WAS THE MAN IN THE MIDDLE, WITH A KIND OF BLACK, SNEERING COOLNESS – CARRYING IT OFF, SIR, REALLY LIKE **SATAN**!"

NO GENTLEMAN BUT WISHES TO **AVOID** A **SCENE**. NAME YOUR FIGURE.

WE SCREWED HIM UP TO A **HUNDRED POUNDS** FOR THE CHILD'S FAMILY. AND WHERE DO YOU THINK HE FETCHED THE MONEY, BUT THAT PLACE WITH THE **DOOR**.

HE WHIPPED OUT A **KEY**, WENT IN AND RETURNED WITH TEN POUNDS IN **GOLD** AND A **CHEQUE** FOR THE BALANCE – SIGNED WITH A **NAME** I CANNOT MENTION.

MY FELLOW WAS A REALLY **DAMNABLE** MAN. BUT THE PERSON THAT DREW THE CHEQUE IS THE VERY PINK OF THE PROPRIETIES, **CELEBRATED** TOO.

BLACKMAIL, I SUPPOSED. AN HONEST MAN PAYING FOR SOME OF THE **CAPERS** OF HIS **YOUTH**.

YOU NEVER ASKED THIS ... OTHER MAN ABOUT THE PLACE WITH THE DOOR?

NO, SIR, I MAKE IT A RULE OF MINE – THE MORE IT LOOKS LIKE **QUEER STREET**, THE LESS I ASK.

AND IF I DO NOT ASK **YOU** THE NAME OF THE OTHER PARTY, ENFIELD, IT IS BECAUSE I KNOW IT ALREADY. BUT WHAT IS THE NAME OF THE MAN WHO WALKED OVER THE CHILD?

HYDE.

EDWARD HYDE.

5

THAT EVENING MR UTTERSON CAME HOME TO HIS BACHELOR HOUSE IN SOMBRE SPIRITS...

IN HIS BUSINESS ROOM HE OPENED HIS SAFE, AND SAT DOWN WITH A CLOUDED BROW TO STUDY ITS CONTENTS...

Dr. Jekyll's Will

TUT!

IN CASE OF THE **DECEASE** OF **HENRY JEKYLL, M.D.,** ALL HIS POSSESSIONS ARE TO PASS INTO THE HANDS OF HIS "FRIEND AND BENEFACTOR – **EDWARD HYDE!**"

AND SHOULD JEKYLL **DISAPPEAR** FOR ANY PERIOD OVER THREE MONTHS, **HYDE** SHOULD STEP INTO JEKYLL'S SHOES WITHOUT FURTHER DELAY!

TUT TUT TUT!

IT WAS BAD ENOUGH WHEN EDWARD HYDE WAS BUT A **NAME** OF WHICH I COULD LEARN NO MORE.

BUT IT IS **WORSE** WHEN HE BEGINS TO BE CLOTHED WITH **DETESTABLE** ATTRIBUTES.

TUT!

AT FIRST I THOUGHT THE WILL WAS **MADNESS.**

NOW I BEGIN TO FEAR IT IS **DISGRACE!**

He set forth in the direction of **CAVENDISH SQUARE** where his friend, the great **DR LANYON**, had his house...

You and I must be the oldest **FRIENDS** that Henry Jekyll has, **LANYON**.

I see little of him now.

It is more than **TEN YEARS** since Jekyll became too **FANCIFUL** for me.

He began to go **WRONG** — wrong in **MIND**, with his **UNSCIENTIFIC BALDERDASH!**

Did you ever come across a **PROTÉGÉ** of his — one Hyde?

No. Never heard of him.

Supposing that Lanyon and Jekyll had differed only on some **POINT** of **SCIENCE**, Utterson returned home...

THERE SPRANG UP IN THE LAWYER'S MIND A SINGULARLY STRONG *CURIOSITY* TO BEHOLD THE FEATURES OF THE *REAL* MR HYDE.

FROM THAT TIME FORWARD, MR UTTERSON BEGAN TO *HAUNT* THE DOOR IN THE BY-STREET OF SHOPS.

IN THE MORNING BEFORE OFFICE HOURS...

IF HE IS TO BE MR HYDE, I SHALL BE MR SEEK!

AT *NOON* WHEN BUSINESS WAS PLENTY AND TIME SCARCE...

AT *NIGHT* UNDER THE FACE OF THE FOGGED CITY MOON...

AND AT LAST, ON A FINE DRY NIGHT WITH FROST IN THE AIR, HIS PATIENCE WAS REWARDED.

MR HYDE, I THINK..?

HYDE SHRANK BACK WITH A HISSING INTAKE OF BREATH...

THAT IS MY NAME.

WHAT DO YOU WANT?

I AM MR UTTERSON, OF GAUNT STREET, AN OLD FRIEND OF DR JEKYLL'S. I THOUGHT YOU MIGHT ADMIT ME...?

YOU WILL NOT FIND JEKYLL. HE IS FROM HOME.

THEN WILL YOU DO ME A FAVOUR? WILL YOU LET ME SEE YOUR FACE?

THE PAIR STARED AT EACH OTHER FIXEDLY...

IT IS AS WELL WE HAVE MET. YOU SHOULD HAVE MY ADDRESS IN SOHO.

AND NOW... HOW DID YOU KNOW ME?

WE HAVE COMMON FRIENDS. JEKYLL, FOR INSTANCE.

HE NEVER TOLD YOU! I DID NOT THINK YOU WOULD HAVE LIED!

NEXT MOMENT, WITH EXTRAORDINARY QUICKNESS, HE HAD DISAPPEARED INTO THE HOUSE.

MY POOR OLD HARRY JEKYLL! IF EVER I READ **SATAN'S SIGNATURE** UPON A FACE, IT IS ON THAT OF YOUR NEW FRIEND!

ROUND THE CORNER FROM THE BY-STREET THERE WAS A SQUARE OF ANCIENT, HANDSOME HOUSES...

IS DR JEKYLL AT HOME, POOLE?

NO, SIR.

I SAW MR HYDE GO IN BY THE OLD **DISSECTING ROOM** DOOR. IS THAT RIGHT?

QUITE RIGHT, SIR.

MR HYDE HAS A **KEY**. ALL THE SERVANTS HAVE ORDERS TO **OBEY** HIM — BUT MOSTLY HE COMES AND GOES BY THE LABORATORY.

JEKYLL WAS **WILD** WHEN HE WAS YOUNG. THIS HYDE MUST BE THE **GHOST** OF SOME **OLD SIN** — PUNISHMENT COMING YEARS AFTER MEMORY HAS FORGOTTEN!

IF HYDE SUSPECTS THE EXISTENCE OF THE WILL, HE MAY GROW **IMPATIENT** TO INHERIT.

POOR HARRY JEKYLL!

A FORTNIGHT LATER, DR JEKYLL GAVE ONE OF HIS PLEASANT DINNERS TO SOME OLD CRONIES, AND MR UTTERSON SO CONTRIVED THAT HE REMAINED BEHIND...

JEKYLL – YOU KNOW THAT **WILL** OF YOURS..?

UTTERSON, I NEVER SAW A MAN SO **DISTRESSED** AS YOU WERE BY MY WILL... UNLESS IT WERE THAT PEDANT, **LANYON**, AT WHAT HE CALLED MY **SCIENTIFIC HERESIES**!

YOU KNOW I NEVER APPROVED OF YOUR WILL. AND NOW... I HAVE BEEN LEARNING SOMETHING OF **YOUNG HYDE**.

WHAT **I** HEARD WAS **ABOMINABLE**.

I DO NOT CARE TO HEAR MORE!

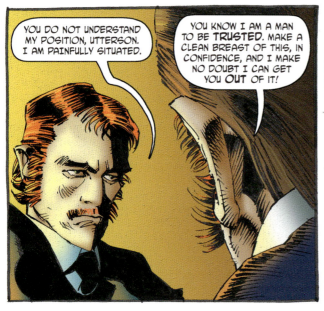

YOU DO NOT UNDERSTAND MY POSITION, UTTERSON. I AM PAINFULLY SITUATED.

YOU KNOW I AM A MAN TO BE **TRUSTED**. MAKE A CLEAN BREAST OF THIS, IN CONFIDENCE, AND I MAKE NO DOUBT I CAN GET YOU **OUT** OF IT!

MY GOOD UTTERSON, I WOULD TRUST YOU BEFORE ANY MAN ALIVE – AYE, BEFORE **MYSELF**, IF I COULD MAKE THE CHOICE.

BUT IT IS NOT SO BAD AS THAT. JUST TO PUT YOUR GOOD HEART AT REST, I WILL TELL YOU **ONE** THING...

THE MOMENT I CHOOSE, I CAN BE **RID** OF MR HYDE. I GIVE YOU MY HAND UPON THAT. I KNOW YOU HAVE SEEN HIM; HE TOLD ME SO; AND I FEAR HE WAS **RUDE**.

BUT I DO SINCERELY TAKE A VERY GREAT **INTEREST** IN THAT YOUNG MAN.

AND IF I AM TAKEN AWAY, UTTERSON, I WISH YOU TO PROMISE THAT YOU WILL BEAR WITH HIM, AND GET HIS **RIGHTS** FOR HIM.

I CAN'T PRETEND THAT I SHALL EVER **LIKE** HIM.

I DON'T ASK THAT. I ONLY ASK FOR **JUSTICE** — FOR YOU TO **HELP** HIM, FOR MY SAKE, WHEN I AM NO LONGER HERE.

I PROMISE.

CHAPTER 4: THE CAREW MURDER CASE

NEARLY A YEAR LATER, LONDON WAS STARTLED BY A *CRIME* OF SINGULAR *FEROCITY*...

A *MAIDSERVANT* IN A HOUSE NOT FAR FROM THE RIVER HAD GONE UPSTAIRS TO BED...

AS SHE SAT BY HER WINDOW, SHE BECAME AWARE OF AN AGED GENTLEMAN WITH WHITE HAIR.

ADVANCING TO MEET HIM WAS ANOTHER, AND VERY SMALL, GENTLEMAN...

THE MAID WAS SURPRISED TO RECOGNISE A CERTAIN *MR HYDE*, WHO HAD ONCE VISITED HER MASTER...

GOOD EVENING, SIR. MAY I MAKE SO BOLD AS TO ASK DIRECTIONS OF YOU..?

ALL OF A SUDDEN HYDE BROKE OUT IN A GREAT FLAME OF *ANGER*, BRANDISHING HIS CANE AND CARRYING ON LIKE A *MADMAN*...

NEXT MORNING, MR UTTERSON WAS CALLED TO THE POLICE STATION...

I AM SORRY TO SAY THIS IS **SIR DANVERS CAREW,** THE MEMBER OF PARLIAMENT! TUT **TUT!**

ACCORDING TO MY WITNESS, THE ATTACKER WAS A MAN CALLED **HYDE.** A PARTICULARLY **SMALL** MAN - AND PARTICULARLY **WICKED**-LOOKING!

AYE. EDWARD HYDE.

BROKEN AND BATTERED AS IT WAS, UTTERSON RECOGNISED THE STICK FOR ONE HE HIMSELF HAD PRESENTED MANY YEARS BEFORE... TO **HENRY JEKYLL!**

COME WITH ME IN MY CAB. I CAN TAKE YOU TO HIS HOUSE!

THE FIRST **FOG** OF THE SEASON – A GREAT CHOCOLATE-COLOURED **PALL** – LOWERED OVER HEAVEN AS THE CAB CRAWLED FROM STREET TO STREET...

HERE, IT WOULD BE **DARK,** LIKE THE BACK-END OF EVENING. THERE WOULD BE A **GLOW** AS OF SOME STRANGE **CONFLAGRATION...**

THE DISMAL QUARTER OF **SOHO,** SEEN UNDER THESE SWIRLING GLIMPSES, SEEMED LIKE A CITY IN A **NIGHTMARE.**

MR HYDE AIN'T HERE NOW. HE WERE IN LATE LAST NIGHT, BUT HE WERE GONE AGAIN IN AN HOUR.

HIS HABITS ARE IRREGULAR. OH YES, VERY IRREGULAR!

HYDE'S ROOMS WERE FURNISHED WITH LUXURY AND GOOD TASTE. BUT...

THEY'VE BEEN RANSACKED!

LOOK - DOCUMENTS HAVE BEEN BURNED!

AND WHAT IS THIS..?

THE FINAL PROOF..!

CHAPTER 5: INCIDENT OF THE LETTER

THE DOCTOR HAD BOUGHT THE HOUSE FROM THE HEIRS OF A CELEBRATED SURGEON, THOUGH JEKYLL HAD CHANGED THE USE OF THE BLOCK AT THE BOTTOM OF THE GARDEN...

LATE IN THE AFTERNOON, UTTERSON FOUND HIS WAY TO JEKYLL'S DOOR, WHERE HE WAS AT ONCE ADMITTED...

IT WAS THE FIRST TIME THAT THE LAWYER HAD BEEN RECEIVED IN THAT PART OF HIS FRIEND'S QUARTERS, AND HE GAZED AROUND WITH A DISTASTEFUL SENSE OF STRANGENESS...

THANK YOU, POOLE.

YOU HAVE HEARD THE NEWS? ABOUT CAREW?

HE WAS MY CLIENT, BUT SO ARE YOU; AND I WANT TO KNOW WHAT I AM DOING.

YOU HAVE NOT BEEN MAD ENOUGH TO CONCEAL THIS FELLOW HYDE?

I SWEAR TO GOD I WILL NEVER SET EYES ON HIM AGAIN! I AM DONE WITH HIM IN THIS WORLD. IT IS ALL AT AN END!

INDEED, HE DOES NOT WANT MY HELP. HE IS QUITE SAFE. MARK MY WORDS – HE WILL NEVER MORE BE HEARD OF!

BUT THERE IS ONE THING YOU MAY ADVISE ME. I HAVE RECEIVED A LETTER, AND I AM AT A LOSS WHETHER I SHOULD SHOW IT TO THE POLICE.

THE LETTER WAS WRITTEN IN AN ODD, UPRIGHT HAND AND SIGNED EDWARD HYDE.

I SHALL KEEP THIS AND SLEEP ON IT.

IT SIGNIFIED THAT DR JEKYLL NEED LABOUR UNDER NO ALARM FOR HIS SAFETY, AS HYDE HAD MEANS OF ESCAPE...

NOW ONE WORD MORE: WAS IT HYDE WHO DICTATED THE TERMS OF YOUR WILL?

19

THE DOCTOR NODDED...

I KNEW IT! HE MEANT TO **MURDER** YOU. YOU HAVE HAD A FINE ESCAPE!

I HAVE HAD WHAT IS FAR MORE TO THE PURPOSE. I HAVE HAD A **LESSON**.

O GOD, WHAT A LESSON I HAVE HAD!

BY-THE-BY, POOLE, THERE WAS A **LETTER** HANDED IN TODAY. WHAT WAS THE **MESSENGER** LIKE?

NOTHING CAME TODAY, SIR. OF THAT I AM CERTAIN.

THIS NEWS SENT OFF THE VISITOR WITH HIS **FEARS RENEWED.** PLAINLY, THE LETTER HAD COME BY THE LABORATORY DOOR. POSSIBLY IT HAD BEEN WRITTEN **IN** JEKYLL'S CABINET.

SPECIAL EDITION! SHOCKING MURDER OF AN M.P.!

CAREW

SELF-RELIANT AS HE WAS BY HABIT, UTTERSON BEGAN TO CHERISH A LONGING FOR ADVICE...

PRESENTLY, HE SAT ON ONE SIDE OF HIS OWN HEARTH WITH MR GUEST, HIS HEAD CLERK, UPON THE OTHER...

THIS MAN HYDE, OF COURSE, IS MAD!

I HAVE A DOCUMENT HERE IN HYDE'S HANDWRITING - A MURDERER'S AUTOGRAPH!

AND THIS IS A DINNER INVITATION FROM DR JEKYLL.

THERE IS A RATHER SINGULAR RESEMBLANCE, SIR. THE TWO HANDS ARE IN MANY POINTS IDENTICAL - ONLY DIFFERENTLY SLOPED.

"WHAT?" THOUGHT UTTERSON. "HENRY JEKYLL FORGE FOR A MURDERER?"

AND HIS BLOOD RAN COLD IN HIS VEINS.

TIME RAN ON. THOUSANDS OF POUNDS WERE OFFERED AS **REWARD**, BUT MR HYDE HAD **DISAPPEARED** AS THOUGH HE HAD NEVER EXISTED.

WANTED FOR MURDER –

– EDWARD HYDE

REWARD

MUCH OF HIS **PAST** WAS UNEARTHED, AND ALL OF IT **DISREPUTABLE**...

TALES CAME OUT OF THE MAN'S **CRUELTY**, AT ONCE SO CALLOUS AND VIOLENT; TALES OF HIS VILE LIFE, AND THE **HATRED** THAT SURROUNDED HIS CAREER...

BUT NOW THAT THAT EVIL INFLUENCE HAD WITHDRAWN, A **NEW LIFE** BEGAN FOR DR JEKYLL. WHILST HE HAD ALWAYS BEEN KNOWN FOR **CHARITIES**, HE WAS NOW NO LESS DISTINGUISHED FOR **RELIGION**...

FOR TWO MONTHS, THE DOCTOR WAS **AT PEACE.**

ON THE 8TH OF JANUARY, UTTERSON HAD DINED AT THE DOCTOR'S WITH A SMALL PARTY. **LANYON** HAD BEEN THERE, AS IN THE OLD DAYS WHEN THE TRIO HAD BEEN **INSEPARABLE FRIENDS...**

BUT ON THE 12TH AND AGAIN ON THE 14TH, THE DOOR WAS **SHUT** AGAINST THE LAWYER...

THE DOCTOR IS CONFINED TO THE HOUSE, SIR, AND IS SEEING NO ONE.

REFUSED SIX TIMES, UTTERSON BETOOK HIMSELF TO DOCTOR LANYON'S...

AND WAS **SHOCKED** AT THE CHANGE IN THE DOCTOR. HE HAD HIS **DEATH-WARRANT** WRITTEN LEGIBLY ON HIS FACE, AND A LOOK THAT SEEMED TO TESTIFY TO SOME DEEP-SEATED **TERROR** OF THE MIND.

I AM A **DOOMED** MAN. I HAVE HAD A **SHOCK**, UTTERSON, AND I SHALL **NEVER** RECOVER!

JEKYLL IS ILL, TOO. HAVE YOU SEEN HIM?

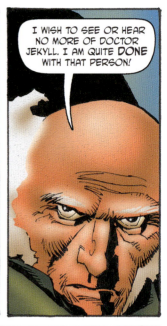

I WISH TO SEE OR HEAR NO MORE OF DOCTOR JEKYLL. I AM QUITE **DONE** WITH THAT PERSON!

TUT TUT!

CAN I NOT DO ANYTHING? WE ARE THREE VERY OLD **FRIENDS**, LANYON.

NOTHING CAN BE DONE.

SOME DAY, UTTERSON, AFTER I AM DEAD, YOU MAY COME TO LEARN THE **RIGHT** AND **WRONG** OF THIS!

IN LESS THAN A FORTNIGHT, DR LANYON WAS **DEAD**...

24

LEAVING UTTERSON A MYSTERIOUS LETTER...

Not to be opened till the death or disappearance of Dr. Henry Jekyll.

HERE AGAIN WERE THE IDEA OF A **DISAPPEARANCE** AND THE NAME OF **JEKYLL** BRACKETED. WHAT IN THE NAME OF GOODNESS COULD IT ALL **MEAN...?**

IT MAY BE DOUBTED IF, FROM THAT DAY FORTH, UTTERSON DESIRED THE SOCIETY OF HIS SURVIVING FRIEND WITH THE SAME EAGERNESS.

HE WENT TO CALL, INDEED, BUT HE WAS PERHAPS **RELIEVED** TO BE DENIED ADMITTANCE TO THAT HOUSE OF VOLUNTARY BONDAGE...

I FEAR I HAVE NO PLEASANT NEWS, SIR.

THE DOCTOR MORE THAN EVER CONFINES HIMSELF TO THE CABINET OVER THE LABORATORY. HE IS OUT OF SPIRITS. HE HAS GROWN **SILENT**.

IT SEEMS AS IF HE HAS SOMETHING ON HIS MIND.

WELL, **THAT** STORY'S AT AN END, AT LEAST. WE SHALL NEVER SEE MORE OF **MR HYDE!**

I HOPE NOT. DID I TELL YOU THAT I ONCE SAW HIM, AND **SHARED** YOUR FEELING OF **REPULSION?**

IMPOSSIBLE TO DO THE ONE WITHOUT THE OTHER!

BY THE WAY, WHAT AN **ASS** YOU MUST HAVE THOUGHT ME, NOT TO KNOW THAT THIS WAS A **BACK** WAY TO JEKYLL'S!

IT CHANCED ON SUNDAY, WHEN MR UTTERSON WAS ON HIS USUAL **WALK** WITH **MR ENFIELD**, THAT THEIR WAY LAY ONCE AGAIN THROUGH THE BY-STREET...

JEKYLL! I TRUST YOU ARE BETTER.

I AM VERY **LOW**, UTTERSON. **VERY** LOW. IT WILL NOT LAST LONG, THANK GOD!

YOU STAY TOO MUCH INDOORS. COME NOW — GET YOUR HAT, AND TAKE A QUICK TURN WITH MR ENFIELD AND ME.

WHY THEN, THE BEST THING WE CAN DO IS SPEAK WITH YOU FROM WHERE WE ARE.

I SHOULD LIKE TO VERY MUCH. BUT NO. NO! IT IS QUITE IMPOSSIBLE. I **DARE** NOT!

I WOULD ASK YOU UP, BUT THE PLACE IS REALLY NOT FIT.

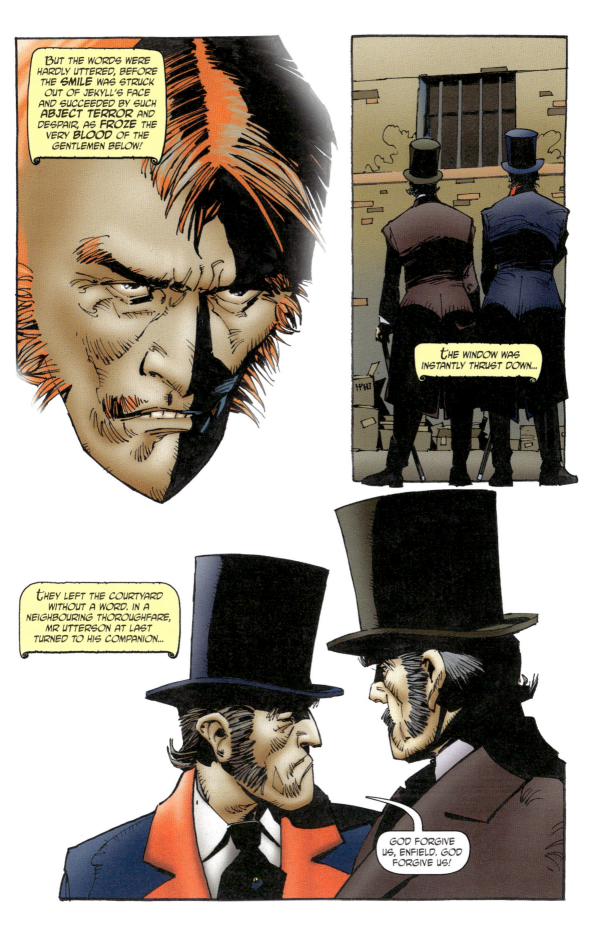

BUT THE WORDS WERE HARDLY UTTERED, BEFORE THE **SMILE** WAS STRUCK OUT OF JEKYLL'S FACE AND SUCCEEDED BY SUCH **ABJECT TERROR** AND DESPAIR, AS **FROZE** THE VERY **BLOOD** OF THE GENTLEMEN BELOW!

THE WINDOW WAS INSTANTLY THRUST DOWN...

THEY LEFT THE COURTYARD WITHOUT A WORD. IN A NEIGHBOURING THOROUGHFARE, MR UTTERSON AT LAST TURNED TO HIS COMPANION...

GOD FORGIVE US, ENFIELD. GOD FORGIVE US!

MR UTTERSON WAS SITTING BY HIS FIRESIDE ONE EVENING, WHEN HE WAS SURPRISED TO RECEIVE A VISIT FROM **POOLE**...

WHAT AILS YOU, MAN? IS THE DOCTOR ILL?

WILL YOU COME ALONG WITH ME AND SEE, SIR?

I THINK THERE'S BEEN **FOUL PLAY**!

CHAPTER 8: THE LAST NIGHT

IT WAS A WILD, COLD SEASONABLE NIGHT OF MARCH, WITH A PALE MOON LYING ON HER BACK.

THE WIND MADE TALKING DIFFICULT, AND FLECKED THE BLOOD INTO THE FACE.

STRUGGLE AS HE MIGHT, THERE WAS BORNE IN UPON UTTERSON'S MIND A **CRUSHING ANTICIPATION** OF CALAMITY.

THE HALL WAS BRIGHTLY LIGHTED UP; THE FIRE WAS BUILT HIGH, AND ABOUT THE HEARTH THE **SERVANTS** STOOD HUDDLED LIKE A FLOCK OF SHEEP...

BLESS GOD! IT'S MR UTTERSON!

THEY ARE ALL **AFRAID**, SIR.

PLEASE, FOLLOW ME, AND YOU MAY LEARN **WHY.**

COME AS GENTLY AS YOU CAN, SIR. I WANT YOU TO **HEAR**, BUT NOT BE **HEARD!**

MR UTTERSON, SIR, ASKING TO SEE YOU.

TELL HIM I CANNOT SEE ANYONE.

WELL, SIR - WAS THAT MY MASTER'S **VOICE**?

IT SEEMS MUCH CHANGED.

CHANGED? HAVE I BEEN **TWENTY YEARS** IN THE DOCTOR'S HOUSE, TO BE **DECEIVED** ABOUT HIS **VOICE**?

NO, SIR! THE DOCTOR'S BEEN MADE AWAY WITH! IT HAPPENED **EIGHT DAYS** AGO, WHEN WE HEARD HIM CRY OUT.

AND **WHO'S** IN THERE INSTEAD OF HIM, AND **WHY** IT STAYS THERE, IS A THING THAT CRIES TO HEAVEN!

SUPPOSING DR JEKYLL TO HAVE BEEN... WELL, **MURDERED**, WHAT COULD INDUCE THE MURDERER TO **STAY**?

ALL WEEK, HIM, OR **IT**, HAS BEEN CRYING NIGHT AND DAY FOR SOME SORT OF **MEDICINE**.

EVERY DAY, OBEYING WRITTEN PAPERS, I HAVE BEEN SENT FLYING TO ALL THE **CHEMISTS** IN TOWN. EVERY TIME I BROUGHT THE STUFF BACK, I WAS ORDERED TO **RETURN** IT BECAUSE IT WAS NOT **PURE**.

THIS DRUG IS WANTED BITTER BAD!

AND WHEN I **SAW** MY MASTER, THE **HAIR** STOOD UPON MY HEAD LIKE **QUILLS**. HE WAS DIGGING AMONG THE CRATES, LOOKING FOR THIS DRUG...

"BUT WHY HAD HE A **MASK** UPON HIS FACE? WHY DID HE CRY OUT LIKE A **RAT**, AND **RUN** FROM HIS LOYAL SERVANT?"

YOUR MASTER IS PLAINLY SEIZED BY ONE OF THOSE MALADIES THAT BOTH **TORTURE** AND **DEFORM** THE SUFFERER. HENCE, THE **ALTERATION** OF HIS **VOICE** – AND THE **MASK** – AND HIS **EAGERNESS** TO FIND THIS DRUG.

THAT... **THING** WAS **NOT** MY MASTER, AND THERE'S THE TRUTH! THIS WAS MORE OF A **DWARF!**

IT IS THE BELIEF OF MY HEART THAT IT WAS **EDWARD HYDE** – AND THAT THERE WAS **MURDER** DONE!

JEKYLL! I **MUST** AND **SHALL** SEE YOU! IF NOT BY FAIR MEANS, THEN BY FOUL!

UTTERSON FOR GOD'S SAKE, HAVE MERCY!

THAT'S NOT JEKYLL'S VOICE! IT'S HYDE'S!

DOWN WITH THE DOOR, POOLE!

THE BESIEGERS, APPALLED BY THEIR OWN RIOT AND THE STILLNESS THAT HAD SUCCEEDED, STOOD BACK AND PEERED IN...

IN THE MIDST THERE LAY THE BODY OF A MAN, SORELY *CONTORTED* AND STILL *TWITCHING*...

EDWARD HYDE!

BY THE CRUSHED PHIAL IN HIS HAND, AND THE STRONG SMELL OF KERNELS... WE ARE LOOKING AT THE BODY OF A *SELF-DESTROYER!*

NOWHERE WAS THERE ANY TRACE OF HENRY JEKYLL, DEAD OR ALIVE.

I MUST GO HOME AND READ THESE DOCUMENTS IN QUIET. BUT I SHALL BE BACK BEFORE MIDNIGHT, POOLE...

WHEN WE SHALL SEND FOR THE *POLICE!*

"ON THE 9TH OF JANUARY, I RECEIVED AN ENVELOPE IN THE HAND OF HENRY JEKYLL..."

Dear Lanyon, My life, my honour, my reason are all at your mercy. If you fail me tonight, I am lost!

Drive straight to my house. You are to enter my cabinet and draw out, with all its contents, the fourth drawer from the top...

At midnight, admit into your house a man who will present himself in my name, and place in his hands the drawer...

WILL YOU SUFFER ME TO TAKE THE GLASS IN MY HAND? YOUR SIGHT SHALL BE BLASTED BY A PRODIGY TO STAGGER THE UNBELIEF OF SATAN!

I HAVE GONE TOO FAR TO PAUSE BEFORE I SEE THE END!

"THERE BEFORE MY EYES — PALE AND SHAKEN, HALF-FAINTING AND GROPING ABOUT LIKE A MAN RESTORED FROM DEATH — STOOD HENRY JEKYLL!"

O GOD! O GOD!

"WHAT HE TOLD ME IN THE NEXT HOUR, I CANNOT BRING MY MIND TO SET ON PAPER. MY SOUL SICKENED AT IT."

"MY LIFE IS SHAKEN TO ITS ROOTS. SLEEP HAS LEFT ME. THE DEADLIEST TERROR SITS BY ME AT ALL HOURS."

"I FEEL THAT MY DAYS ARE NUMBERED, AND I MUST DIE."

CHAPTER 10:
HENRY JEKYLL'S FULL STATEMENT OF THE CASE

I WAS BORN TO A LARGE **FORTUNE**, ENDOWED BESIDES WITH EXCELLENT PARTS, INCLINED BY NATURE TO **INDUSTRY**; THUS, WITH EVERY GUARANTEE OF AN **HONOURABLE** AND **DISTINGUISHED** FUTURE.

INDEED, THE **WORST** OF MY **FAULTS** WAS A CERTAIN **IMPATIENT GAIETY** OF DISPOSITION, HARD TO RECONCILE WITH MY IMPERIOUS DESIRE TO CARRY MY HEAD HIGH.

HENCE, I **CONCEALED** MY **PLEASURES**, AND WHEN I REACHED YEARS OF REFLECTION, I STOOD ALREADY COMMITTED TO A PROFOUND **DUPLICITY** OF LIFE.

MY **SCIENTIFIC STUDIES** SHED A STRONG LIGHT ON THIS **DUAL NATURE**. WITH EVERY DAY, I DREW STEADILY NEARER TO THE TRUTH...

THAT MAN IS **NOT** TRULY **ONE**, BUT TRULY **TWO**.

IF EACH ELEMENT COULD BE HOUSED IN **SEPARATE IDENTITIES**, THE **UNJUST** MIGHT GO HIS WAY, DELIVERED FROM THE **REMORSE** OF HIS MORE UPRIGHT TWIN...

AND THE **JUST** COULD DO THE GOOD THINGS IN WHICH HE FOUND HIS PLEASURE, NO LONGER EXPOSED TO **DISGRACE** BY THIS EXTRANEOUS EVIL.

I MANAGED TO COMPOUND A **DRUG** BY WHICH THESE POWERS SHOULD BE DETHRONED FROM THEIR SUPREMACY, AND LATE ONE ACCURSED NIGHT I DRANK THE SOLUTION...

THE MOST RACKING PAINS SUCCEEDED: A GRINDING IN THE BONES, DEADLY NAUSEA, AND A HORROR OF THE SPIRIT...

I FELT YOUNGER, LIGHTER, HAPPIER. AND I KNEW MYSELF TO BE MORE WICKED – TENFOLD MORE WICKED!

THESE AGONIES SWIFTLY SUBSIDED, AND I CAME TO MYSELF AS IF OUT OF A GREAT SICKNESS.

ALL HUMAN BEINGS ARE COMMINGLED OUT OF GOOD AND EVIL. EDWARD HYDE, ALONE IN THE RANKS OF MANKIND, WAS PURE EVIL!

HAD I APPROACHED MY DISCOVERY IN A MORE NOBLE SPIRIT, FROM THESE AGONIES I HAD COME FORTH AN ANGEL INSTEAD OF A FIEND. BUT NOW I HAD BUT TO DRINK THE CUP TO ASSUME, LIKE A THICK CLOAK, THE BODY OF EDWARD HYDE!

THE PLEASURES WHICH I MADE HASTE TO SEEK IN MY DISGUISE WERE UNDIGNIFIED; BUT IN THE HANDS OF HYDE THEY SOON BEGAN TO TURN TOWARDS THE MONSTROUS...

TWO MONTHS BEFORE THE MURDER OF DANVERS CAREW, I WOKE IN BED WITH ODD SENSATIONS. I HAD GONE TO SLEEP AS **HENRY JEKYLL**...

BUT I HAD **AWAKENED** AS **EDWARD HYDE**!

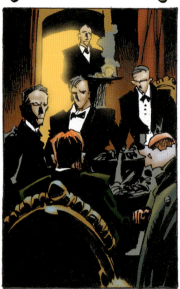

I WAS SLOWLY LOSING HOLD OF MY ORIGINAL AND BETTER SELF. SO I BADE **FAREWELL** TO MY SECRET PLEASURES, AND FOR **TWO MONTHS** I LIVED ONLY AS HENRY JEKYLL...

I BEGAN TO BE **TORTURED** BY THROES AND LONGINGS, AS OF HYDE STRUGGLING AFTER **FREEDOM**. AT LAST, IN AN HOUR OF MORAL WEAKNESS, I AGAIN COMPOUNDED THE DRAUGHT...

MY **DEVIL** HAD LONG BEEN **CAGED**; HE CAME OUT **ROARING**. I MAULED CAREW'S UNRESISTING BODY, TASTING **DELIGHT** FROM EVERY BLOW...

I FLED FROM THE SCENE, GLORYING AND TREMBLING, MY **LUST OF EVIL** GRATIFIED AND STIMULATED...

I WAS NOW CONFINED TO THE BETTER PART OF MY EXISTENCE; LET **HYDE** PEEP OUT FOR BUT AN **INSTANT**, AND THE HANDS OF ALL MEN WOULD BE RAISED TO **SLAY** HIM!

THERE COMES AN END TO ALL THINGS. SEATED IN REGENT'S PARK ON A FINE JANUARY DAY, A **QUALM** CAME OVER ME, A HORRID **NAUSEA** AND THE MOST DEADLY **SHUDDERING**...

I WAS ONCE MORE EDWARD HYDE!

IF I SOUGHT TO ENTER MY HOUSE, MY OWN SERVANTS WOULD CONSIGN ME TO THE **GALLOWS**. I SAW I MUST EMPLOY ANOTHER HAND - AND THOUGHT OF **LANYON**.

FROM THAT DAY FORTH, IT WAS ONLY UNDER THE IMMEDIATE STIMULATION OF THE DRUG THAT I WAS ABLE TO WEAR THE COUNTENANCE OF JEKYLL. IF I **SLEPT**, OR EVEN **DOZED** FOR A MINUTE, IT WAS AS **HYDE** THAT I AWAKENED!

I BECAME WEAK IN BOTH BODY AND MIND... AND THE POWERS OF HYDE SEEMED TO **GROW** WITH THE **SICKLINESS** OF JEKYLL.

MY PUNISHMENT MIGHT HAVE GONE ON FOR **YEARS**, BUT FOR THE LAST CALAMITY WHICH HAS NOW FALLEN: PROVISION OF THE **DRUG** HAS BEGUN TO RUN **LOW**. I SENT OUT **POOLE** FOR FRESH SUPPLY - AND IT WAS WITHOUT **EFFICACY**.

I AM NOW PERSUADED THAT MY FIRST SUPPLY WAS **IMPURE**, AND IT WAS THAT **IMPURITY** WHICH LENT EFFICACY TO THE DRAUGHT!

I AM FINISHING THIS STATEMENT UNDER THE INFLUENCE OF THE **LAST** OF THE **OLD POWDERS**. THIS, THEN, IS THE LAST TIME THAT **HENRY JEKYLL** CAN THINK HIS OWN THOUGHTS, OR SEE HIS OWN FACE...

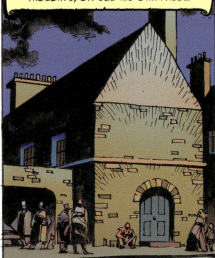

DOOM IS CLOSING ON US. HALF AN HOUR FROM NOW, WHEN I SHALL AGAIN AND FOR EVER REINDUE THAT HATED PERSONALITY, I KNOW I SHALL SIT **SHUDDERING** AND **WEEPING** IN MY CHAIR...

WILL HYDE **DIE** UPON THE **SCAFFOLD?** OR WILL HE FIND THE **COURAGE** TO **RELEASE** HIMSELF AT THE LAST MINUTE?

HERE, THEN, AS I LAY DOWN THE PEN, AND PROCEED TO SEAL UP MY CONFESSION, I BRING THE LIFE OF THAT UNHAPPY HENRY JEKYLL TO AN END.

THE END

Robert Louis Stevenson

(1850–1894)

Robert Louis Stevenson was born in Edinburgh in 1850. His family wanted him to become a civil engineer, as the family business was lighthouse engineering. But Robert's imagination was filled with images of romantic and heroic deeds. His interests did not lie in the science of building lighthouses, but more in the adventure held by the seas they illuminated and by the lands he had yet to explore.

By way of a compromise, he studied law at Edinburgh University and finished his degree, but by the time he reached his twenties he knew that his real passion was writing.

Stevenson suffered all his life from a serious lung disease, and he travelled constantly in search of a climate that would help him get better. He wrote about his experiences in *The Silverado Squatters* (1883), and in his very popular book *Travels with a Donkey in the Cévennes* (1879).

Despite his worsening health, he continued to remain optimistic in spirit and write as much as he could. In fact, in the following years he produced much of his best-known and best-loved work. He had a great success with a novel, *Treasure Island* (1883) which became immensely popular. In 1886, he wrote *Kidnapped*, which became a great favourite and was quickly established as a classic. It was followed by a sequel, *Catriona*, also known as *David Balfour*, (1893), and *The Master of Ballantrae* (1889). Stevenson also wrote poetry, and his most successful poetry book was *A Child's Garden of Verses* (1885).

In 1885, he published a dark thriller about the duality of human nature and the struggle between good and evil – *Strange Case of Dr Jekyll and Mr Hyde*. This book, on which this graphic novel is based, established him as a great writer. The story is said to have initially been written in a frenzied three days. Though some scholars disagree, the story goes that he consigned this first version to the fire and started it again. In a further three days' time he had created anew the allegorical novella with which we are familiar today. A classic tale that has passed into the modern psyche.

In 1888, Stevenson, his American wife, Fanny Osbourne, and his family headed for the South Pacific. There they visited a leper colony at Molokai which inspired him to write *Father Damien: An Open Letter to the Reverend Dr Hyde of Honolulu* (1890) in tribute to the Belgian priest who devoted his life to the venture. Stevenson settled in Samoa, which helped him regain his health to some degree. Sadly, he died in 1894 of a brain haemorrhage while still working on *Weir of Hermiston* (published unfinished, 1896). The next day, Samoan chieftains honoured Stevenson, their "Tusitala" or "storyteller", with a burial site on top of Mount Vaea, and he was carried there over several miles on the shoulders of the natives.

Some say Stevenson created some of the most memorable fiction in the English language. His immense popularity with readers made 20th-century scholars unfairly scathing of his talent but his reputation continues to grow. He can count amongst his admirers Ernest Hemingway, Rudyard Kipling, Vladimir Nabokov, GK Chesterton, Henry James, and Joseph Conrad. He is popular with modern readers and his reputation continues to grow today.

Illustration courtesy Illustrated London News.

Alan Grant

Alan Grant is an internationally acclaimed writer of graphic novels and comic strips who has been writing for that industry for nearly 30 years. He always had a love of comics, even as a child, learning to read at his granny's knee with the help of *The Beano* and *The Dandy*.

Alan worked as an editor for DC Thomson, the Scottish publisher of those titles, in 1967, where he met fellow editor, and future *Judge Dredd* collaborator, John Wagner. For a time he worked as a freelance writer of girls' romantic stories. It was not until 1979, when John Wagner asked him to write his first story for a UK comic called *Starlord*, that he finally got to do his dream job, working for comic books like those he read as a teenager.

The *Starlord* story got him noticed by *2000AD*. Later that same year, he was hired by them as an assistant editor. It was at *2000AD* that he was to make his name. He left them after around two years to pursue a freelance career, and started collaborating with John Wagner. During their thirteen-year working partnership they wrote *Judge Dredd*, *Strontium Dog*, *Robo-Hunter* and *Ace Trucking Co.* for *2000AD*; *Doomlord, Joe Soap Private Eye* and *Computer Warrior* for *The Eagle*; *The Outsiders* for DC Comics; *Nightbreed* and *The Last American* for Epic; and *The Bogie Man* series, based in Glasgow, which is still the highest-selling British independent comic.

Grant's involvement with *Judge Dredd* has lasted over 25 years and together with John Wagner he created hundreds of stories for what became *2000AD*'s most popular strip.

When the Grant/Wagner partnership ended, Alan worked on titles as varied as *Detective Comics*; *Batman* for DC comics, which he wrote for over a decade; *Lobo*; *L.E.G.I.O.N. '89*; *Legends of the Dark Knight*; and *The Demon*. More recently, he has written *Anderson Psi Division* and *Young Middenface* for *Judge Dredd Megazine*; *Robo-Hunter* for *2000AD*; and the sequel to *The Authority/Lobo* for DC/Wildstorm. In 2007, commissioned by Edinburgh UNESCO City of Literature Trust, he embarked on his first adaptation of a classic novel, creating with long-time collaborator, artist Cam Kennedy, a highly acclaimed graphic novel version of Robert Louis Stevenson's *Kidnapped*, published by Waverley Books. *Strange Case of Dr Jekyll and Mr Hyde* is Grant's second classic adaptation and Grant and Kennedy's second title together with Waverley Books.

Alan lives in Moniaive in Dumfries and Galloway with his wife Sue where they organise the yearly Moniaive Comics Festival, now in its fourth year.

Cam Kennedy

Cam Kennedy has been working in the comics industry since 1967 and is one of the most respected artists in the business. He started work as a commercial artist, working in his home town of Glasgow and also in London. In 1967, Cam went freelance and started working for DC Thomson's *Commando* comics. He worked on *Commando* titles until 1972 when he moved to France for 6 years, working as a fine artist.

When Cam returned to Scotland in 1978 he once again returned to working on comics. He sent some drawings to *Battle* comic and was asked to work on *Fighting Mann*. *2000AD* noticed his work on *Battle*, liked it and approached him to work on their strip *Rogue Trooper*. Soon after that he got the opportunity to work on what would become, arguably, his most famous strip, *Judge Dredd*. He is also well known for his work on *The VCs*, also for *2000AD*, not forgetting the *Future Shocks* short strips and pin-ups that he has created for that title.

Over the years Cam has worked with all the major American publishers, his first American job being for DC Comics pencilling the series *Outcasts*. In 1988, Cam worked with Tom Veitch on their series *The Light and Darkness War* for Epic comics. A few years later Cam again worked with Tom Veitch on the hugely popular Dark Horse series *Dark Empire* and *Dark Empire II*. His work on these titles virtually relaunched the *Star Wars* franchise in comic form. His artwork for *Dark Empire* seemed to revive a nostalgia in

Star Wars fans for the original films. Since then, Cam has regularly created artwork for many American titles including *Boba Fett*, *Lobo* and *Punisher*.

Cam has been working, on-and-off, with Alan Grant for around 30 years, from his first days on *Judge Dredd* to their present work with Waverley Books. In 1990, he worked with Alan and John Wagner on *Unamerican Gladiators* featuring the popular character, Lobo. That same year the trio produced a Nick Fury story *Greetings from Scotland*. They collaborated again in 1991 on The Punisher story *Blood on the Moors*. Cam's first stint on Batman in 1992 was with John Wagner in *A Gotham Tale* and then in 1993 he worked again with Alan and John on the Batman/Dredd crossover *Vendetta in Gotham*.

In 2007, Cam's artwork for the *Kidnapped* graphic novel, commissioned by Edinburgh UNESCO City of Literature Trust as part of their One Book–One Edinburgh campaign, was highly acclaimed and is now to be found in the National Library of Scotland. He joins Alan Grant and Waverley Books once again to create *Strange Case of Dr Jekyll and Mr Hyde*.

Cam lives and works in Orkney where he has stayed for 27 years. He claims every time he tries to leave the place the weather is too bad to make the crossing.

Photograph: Copyright Ian MacNicol.

Robert Louis Stevenson's *Strange Case of Dr Jekyll and Mr Hyde* – The Graphic Novel

Published 2016 by Waverley Books
Waverley Books is an imprint of The Gresham Publishing Company, Ltd.,
Academy Park, Building 4000, Gower Street,
Glasgow, G51 1PR, Scotland, UK.

First printed 2008.
Reprinted 2014, 2016.

Adapted text © 2008 Alan Grant.
Illustrations © 2008 Cam Kennedy

ISBN: 978-1-902407-44-9

Scanning by Castle Quoy Graphics & Design, Stromness, Orkney KW16 3AW
Colourist and letterer – Jamie Grant, Hope Street Studios, Glasgow G2 6AB

Photographs of Cam Kennedy and Alan Grant © Ian MacNicol

Printed and bound in the EU,
by Drukarnia Skleniarz, Kraków, Poland

WAVERLEY
BOOKS

www.waverley-books.co.uk
info@waverley-books.co.uk
Find us on [f] facebook/pages/waverleybooks